D1560685

poetry

Issue XIV | Summer 2022

Nightingale & Sparrow

Juliette Sebock, Editor-in-Chief
Copyright *Nightingale & Sparrow* 2020
ISSN 2642-0104 (print)
ISSN 2641-7693 (online)
nightingaleandsparrow.com

Cover Image by Karen Pierce Gonzalez, "Black Swan"

Contents

VISUAL ART

CONTRIBUTORS BIOGRAPHIES

ISSUE STAFF

Nightingale and Sparrow
Juliette Sebock

Eternal optimist
flying high above the pain,
floating over orchard walls,
away from life, away from here,

banished to the sky
in a prison of restraint,
free from orchard branches, jailhouse bars,
in flight where poachers, gatekeepers can't reach you.

Still, never still,
fleeing the fears you should have left behind;
nightingale and sparrow in an urgent race
against life, against fear, against time.

Letter from the Editor

Dear Reader,

Thank you for picking up our latest issue of *Nightingale & Sparrow Literary Magazine*! This is our fourteenth issue and, as has become the norm over the past several years, was not brought about without its share of strife.

This quarterly theme is one that holds a special place in my heart. Poetry is where I got my own start in the literary world (feel free to check out *Mistakes Were Made* at your favourite bookseller for a trip in that Delorean). Poetry is the form I turn to when life is at its darkest and at its brightest. *poetry*, then, has to be something special.

For this issue, we provided the following prompt: "...send us your poems, prose, and visual art masterpieces with poetic qualities. Bring us rhythm, rhyme, and sonnets turned into stories. Transform couplets into cross-stitch, stanzas into sculptures, or poems into paintings. Show just how interdisciplinary your favourite form can be." With a bit of clarification to ensure we received submissions from our other genres, this theme slowly came to life.

From "With the Birds Again" by Alexander Etheridge and "An autistic reflects on friendship with trees, lakes, and certain birds" by Margaret King to Amanda McLeod's "Languages Where Green And Blue Are One Colour" and Karen Pierce Gonzalez's "Enchanted Forest," you'll find poetry both literal and figurative within these pages.

As always, our most sincere thanks to the N&S team, our submitters and contributors, readers, customers, and other supporters who make all things *Nightingale & Sparrow* possible.

Enjoy these moments of *poetry*.

Juliette Sebock
Editor-in-Chief, *Nightingale & Sparrow*

Leading up to the launch of each issue of our literary magazine, Nightingale & Sparrow showcases a series of themed micropoems across social media.

poetry micropoem selections include:

POETRY

The Open Door

Rob McKinnon

Red geraniums bloom
in the front garden
otherwise choking with weeds.

Rotting junk mail
stuffed into the filled letter box
hangs precariously
waiting to join other remnants
already on the ground.

White paint flakes from the front bay window
as faded curtains droop unevenly
falling off their rings.

Filled dusty cardboard boxes
on a broken cloth couch
crams under the front veranda.

The open front door held ajar by a shoe
exposes the filling clutter in the hallway
seen from the footpath through the geraniums
and acts as an escape route
for the melodic piano notes
played with pounding passion
accompanying the crescendo of a symphony
booming in the background.

Street traffic rattles passed
not paying any attention.

quiet, quiet, quiet

John C. Polles

Trigger Warning: isolation, anxiety, depression

Waves crash—

Saltwater drenches west
ward face of dying light
house, rusted iron cage,
just like in that movie—

A safe harbor?
Or a bleak omen?

I, alone inside and folded in
ward upon myself, wait...
for what?

A safe harbor or
a bleak omen?

It gets dark early this
far north, you know,
this time of year—

Bleak omen,
safe harbor?

What do they want from me,
here and now,
what are they looking for?

Safe harbor?

Here and now,
alone and inward,
folded into
quiet, quiet, quiet
cocooned shadows,
I wonder,
again,
as wrought
iron window frames
clatter—

With the Birds Again

Alexander Etheridge

Every Time here in the dense brush at twilight,
little birds all chatter at once—they know dark

comes on slowly, bringing with it shreds
of eternity. They know a road to the shadows of

Heaven stretches out in us like a secret. *This
is the waking fable*, they say, *this is the living*

memory our memories forget. Night opens around us
like a charcoal drawing, and the dusty sparrows

grow still as the ruins of an ancient cathedral.
Joy is clustered with grief inside us, and our prayers

blow softly apart like pollen grains. We follow a path
to the last leaves, and we know death begins slowly,

down in the roots. We're linked by a thread of fear
and hope. A hailstorm moves from heart to heart—

But an unseen light shepherds us, even through agonies
and decay, something elemental in us watches

the moons of God. We walk out over black and stony
riverbeds, imagining a kinder world. Through the hunger

and desolation we remember an April dream
the forest had, and our faith is swept clean

of doubt. The birds fly out once more, quiet as stars,
older and each alone—purer and peaceful again.

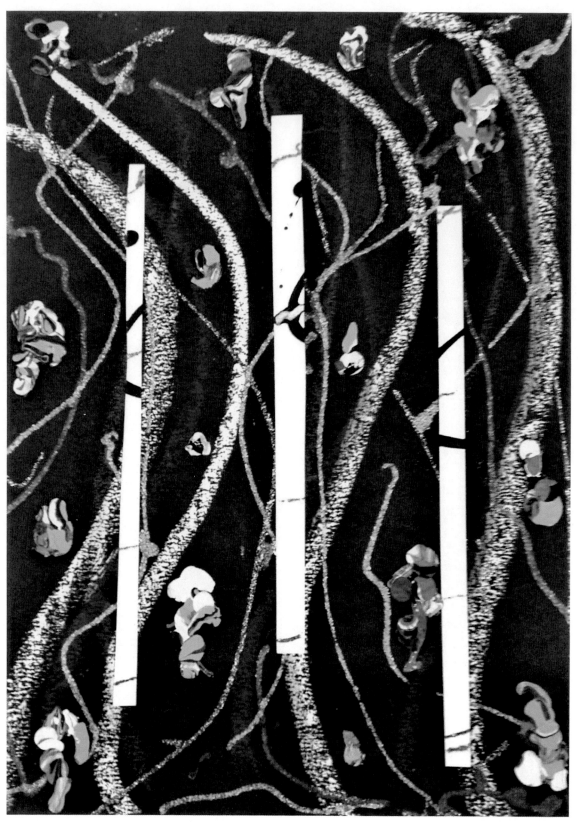

Enchanted Forest
Karen Pierce Gonzalez

Astronomy Two Ways

John Rodzvilla

Most stars move about for an hour
Before pointing their rough heads home,
But not the Plough, never the Plough.

The Plough isn't ever up in
The evening, even though it
Weighs under a gram.

The Plough is part of a
Constellation called the
Great Bear.

It loafs and eases into to
Wintry night before falling
In line with the other stars.

2.
Most stars move around and
Shake their asses toward evening,
All for the attention of the Plough.

The Plough has never
Handled anything under
A gram, he always sold weight.

The moon landed on heads;
Time is up. Game called.

The Plough is out of a constellation called
Great Bear, which serves winter evenings.

Fallen

Richard LeDue

On a page, words fall,
less valuable than loose change,
unless accepted
by a paying publication-
then the "p" in poem grows up,
and the poet vindicated
for dropping chemistry classes
to study sonnets written by the dead.

"Yet are they truly gone?"
muses a professor, who wrote
about the view from the plane,
flying over Chinese landscapes,
only to get a contributor's copy,
eventually forsakened to the bottom
of a cardboard box during a yard sale
after the estate was settled.

Medusa

Sandy Benitez

In the courtyard,
I fed you grapes
fresh from the vine.
Poured you boysenberry wine
and scrubbed your dirty feet
until they were pink
as cherry blossoms.

Later, I noticed you sketching
nude figures of women;
their breasts ripe and supple
legs spread wide
revealing desire
in shapes of irises,
furry halved peaches.

Hesitantly, I asked you
why you didn't draw me.
You replied that you'd seen
enough of me to sate your interest.
Was I that ordinary?
Or did I remind you
of a modern day Medusa,
shaking her reptilian curls
whenever a bad mood arose.

But there was only one monster here.
Mirrors inhabited the empty spaces,
moving faces from wall to wall.
You had looked my way
enough times through the years
and not once did you ever
turn to stone.

Pine Burst

Karen Pierce Gonzalez

Hiraeth

Grant Howington

Trigger Warning: Violence Suicide

the poets have been hanged from trees tonight
each one a gutted salt-cured gar tonight
their legs move to the wind's sweet tune tonight
like paired-off ballerinas for tonight
while bending branches sway in step tonight
enchanted by the dancing dead tonight
again I'll sneak into your room tonight
so I can beg you to come out tonight
tomorrow clouds might burst but not tonight
they only leak a bit of piss tonight
because they're pregnant with spring rain tonight
and since the poets are strung-up tonight
let's kiss beneath their kicking feet tonight

swaddled in narrow strips of starless sky

The Daisies Miss Me

Leslie Cairns

I grew up on Amber Way, where the tree fell on my Dad's Chevrolet but it somehow ran. & back then I ran and swerved – left behind – past rocks big as kindergartners, thinking that I had all the summers in the world to obtain scabbed knees. I sat there, folded over, and wondered if the daisies missed me in between.

Then, I outgrow the worn down moss carpet, the pine wood for the ceilings. Now, I think of that place, and don't think of home. Squinching eyes, instead, I think of friends in sleeping bags, staring up at the tree colored ceilings, asking how we breathe in homes of trees–

So then I renamed the next place I went. A ranch house placed near Amish farm pies, and skies that stretched tight with either blizzards or blustery sunburns. & I learned how to tattoo my roots with something akin to tending. Peeling down the blisters on my fingers, tending to the plants planted in perfect rows near the hummingbirds, beaks open and biting for nectar–

& then I outgrew it. Dashed and revolted, drove an ambling car to the mountains, like we all do
When we need to see the steering wheel go on autopilot, climb to cruising speed,
And stay the same for miles.

I haven't renamed this place yet,
When the skies bruise, magenta and magnolia orbs flickering in my vision,
The tears mixing in my bedding and my concrete like confetti–
I'll know it's time to bloom again.

Rains Me

John Grey

It rains me blind,
drowns the city,
this submerged body
of gasping concrete,
gurgling steel.

The world's a shipwreck
sinking in the deep,
broken on rocks of thunder,
mainsails seared by lightning.

I look at my watch,
the one thing visible.
You said 10.00 under the awnings
of the bank.
But there is no bank.
And time, splattered and misting up,
is barely holding on.

It rains me worried.
It rains me stupid.
Such a roiling ocean.
Did the big waves pull you under?

No, here you are,
struggling down Poseidon's sidewalk.
I pull you into me,
hug you close.
It's a perilous night.
Even the life rafts need saving.

A Found Poem from a Never Returned Book
Jeffrey Yamaguchi

CREATIVE NONFICTION

Bundles of Three

K. Gene Friedman

Curbside, daytime hazard lights delimit a polished log loitering parallel to parked cars, a personal injury lawsuit in repose; metal threaded through its pliant core like graphite bloating the gut of an analog pencil. The evenness and imagination of a lonesome Tinker Toy, I squat bedside to interrogate its destiny: a dry-cleaning ticket stapled to its spiral of years à la Paddington Bear's duffle coat, wine cork toggles fastening, cardstock luggage tag dangling... *Please look after...*

Brierfield, Alabama—its origin, embryology, infancy. *2/50*—its order, as if second in a run of fifty fine art prints, separated at birth, limited edition. *PECO*—its owner, a fledgling utility pole it is to be raised by a provider of electricity that falters in the sweat of droning accordion window units and slushy popsicles. Be mindful of your refrigerator door, your outlets to the external; conserve the pockets of cold you harbor.

Under late-stage capitalism, the A/S/L of West Philly's Facebook group:

49th and Larchwood: lights flickering.

51st and Spruce: power back on.

The scattershot shuffle of resource redistribution:

Anyone got space for me to store my insulin at?

Ready to dive!? Whole Foods employees hauling cases of freezer food out back.

An improbable journey—spanning seven states—to support an elevated highway of power lines. I envision the bedraggled tree: dismantled, decapitated, dismembered, filed to fit the geometry of the pencil box truck; claws clenching the sapped Southern soil. Its forty-nine siblings: stapled, seat belted into place. Flakey scales of grout brown and burnt sienna stripped off like guilty fingerprints; mummified corpses laid to rest along grimy West Philadelphian sidewalks.

The cultural anthropologist I'm dating, who will not be defined by labels, is taken by *Pinus palustris*, otherwise known as the *longleaf pine*—a species of evergreen distinguished by needles in bundles of three, its grisly history. Used as tar, pitch, and turpentine for naval ships; now, lumber for suburban development. Its once dominant community supplanted in shoulder-to-shoulder forests where wildfires cannot sweep to clear out competition.

Together, we locate *Brierfield* on his laptop screen, plus- and minus-sign in and out of the region, straddle a Google Earth satellite and soar. Our summer limbs stuck to the tattered sleeping bag sheeting his hand-me-down floor mattress. In the swampy, second-story bedroom where he will not avail of A/C. Out of deference to bug mating calls, the harmonic convergence of male and female mosquito flight tones.

Below: a bounty of Baptist churches, forests identified as plantations, a coal mine museum catalogued in the *Register of Landmarks & Heritage*. Clouds of Pine canopies looming on slanted thickets like crooked rain. The dense grids of wooden pegs, planted to be plucked from the land, reminding of the solitaire boards that occupied me as an only child at a family-style restaurant in *Nowhereville, Pennsylvania*. Where the owners had likely tired of replenishing snapped crayons, tear-off placemats: probably also of *Alabama*—their embryology, infancy.

A Flowing Drop Suspended In Time, Still Flowing

Daniel Rabuzzi

"The point is that all that is intermediate in the ordinary run of things is made immediate; which is what we mean when we say that breathing becomes breathless, hope becomes terror, or time stands still, but without any cessation, in any of these cases, of life, faith, or motion, and with an access of inward, of mutual verisimilitude."

--- R.P. Blackmur, "*The Sacred Fount*" (originally published 1942; reprinted in Blackmur, *Studies in Henry James*, edited with an introduction by Veronica A. Makowsky, New Directions 1983, page 60).

Decades ago: a Green Heron hunts / hunted / is hunting in a half-strangled stream – a dwindled thread at the bottom of a drainage ditch – mere yards from a major intersection in Boston, Massachusetts. The blazing yoke of its eye! The striations of its throat plumage (it must have been an immature), the delicate fronding of the feathers on its back as it leaned forward, coppery green plumes overlapping with the rusty brown, quiet subtle blazonry, imprinting themselves on the space between us. Crouching down among the reeds and minor willows crowding the culvert, my errand evaporated, I tracked the heron as it tracked fish, for many minutes…ten, fifteen, more, I did not know, so cannot remember the specific count, just the unbounded wholeness of the *durée*. The heron had been there always, picking its way over pebbles and twigs, when I appeared. I had always been there at the intersection as trucks roared by, when the heron manifested. The tableau of heron hunting flowed past me along a helical stream-bed. I became the moment, the heron, in the bedraggled stream; its "light, color, depth… awakens an echo in my body," as Merleau-Ponty said about the workings of the eye and the mind.[i] The heron's eye was / is / will be my eye, its minnow-hunger lodged also in my belly.

I have not lived in Boston for many years but I visit often and have, on occasion, passed that intersection. I always pause and look, hoping to catch another glimpse of a Green Heron there, professionally going about its business. I never have (not there, though often enough elsewhere), but I see always the palest tint of a shadow stalking down the little stream; I luxuriate in its "sense of presence and achronological pungency," as Reinhart Koselleck described another multivalent episode.[ii] I smile and am for one prolonged moment in the past, while simultaneously also in the past-as-I-recreate-it, the present, the present-as-I-imagine-it-for-the-future, the future, and the future-in-which-I-am-remembering-my-recollection-of-the-original-event. A gaze, a gasp, a gesture that anchors itself in a place in the world, in the mind, in the world-as-the-mind-constructs-it, the heron was / is / will be ever-present in the water-tables of my mind. Time drops, unspools, concatenates. Drop-Time: when the Green Heron walks with delicate ferocity through my memory, picking a path in the present, already present in the future. Drop-Time: when my mind is the Green Heron's, a study in patience, a shape of hunting. Drop-Time: a surprise and an awakening, time hollowed out from the regular river, elongated and linked across the long stretches of current, directly tied like a bundle of leaves (or feathers) floating and bobbing and dipping in the stream. Drop-Time: in-collapsing and bursting outward at the same time, an imperfect progressive tense (the progressive implausible, the progressive heteroclite?), the aorist essence, *passado no acabado*, entanglements falling under the heading of what Carlo Rovelli calls "the inadequacy of grammar."[iii] The heron in the ditch by the intersection made / makes real the words of T. S. Eliot: "Time present and time past /Are both perhaps present in time future,/And time future contained in time past." [iv] Unaware of Rovelli, of Eliot, uncaring of ontology or entropy, indifferent to chronotopes, the little Green Heron continues the hunt for darters along a tiny brook, then and now embodying and in our future embodied.

[i]   Maurice Merleau-Ponty, "Eye and Mind," in *The Merleau-Ponty Aesthetics Reader*, ed. Galen Johnson; translation by Carleton Dallery from 1961 original (Evanston, IL: Northwestern University Press, 1993), page 125.

[ii]   Reinhart Koselleck, *Futures Past: On the Semantics of Historical Time*, translation by Keith Tribe from 1979 original (Cambridge, MA: MIT University Press, 1990), page 5.

[iii]   Carlo Rovelli, *The Order of Time,* translation by Erica Segre and Simon Carnell from 2017 original (NYC: Riverhead Books, 2018), pages 105-115.

[iv]   T.S. Eliot, "Burnt Norton" in his *Four Quartets* (1936).

An autistic reflects on friendship with trees, lakes, and certain birds

Margaret King

"Cantankerous and untrusting of people, he preferred the company of his cows, feeding them apples by hand and sleeping next to them....Woodward once had an ox named Old Duke who he taught to shake hands and roll over like a dog. 'I loved him,' Hall wrote, 'and I could feel his affection for me.'"

— Steve Edwards, "Misunderstanding Thoreau: Reading Neurodiversity in Literature and in Life"

"When people were able to see trees or the sky, or hear birds, feelings of loneliness fell by 28%."

— "Contact with nature in cities reduces loneliness, study shows," The Guardian, 12/20/21

The lakeshore is beautiful in all seasons, even in the depths of winter. Even on the cloudy and rainy and stormy and especially the snowy days, it is beautiful because it is wild. Sometimes autistics have been thought of as feral people who have never been fully domesticated into our society.[i]

Mid-December, inching towards solstice, we walk back toward the light. Although I'm hundreds of feet above them, their voices carried at least half a mile offshore. I walked to the edge of the steep bluff, and there they were, far below--50 or so geese bobbing on the waves, talking. Were they complaining about the weather? Or were they, like me, worshiping the sun that day?

How few people were out that day making their endless noise, or breathing fresh air, or listening to the crashing waves. A few small children screeched at a nearby playground, but their shrieks did not grate. Joyful sounds felt acceptable, and mingled with the waves and the geese. Although, there was a man walking a dog on that splendid Sunday, blasting a football game out of a radio as he walked. And there was another man, half a mile up, sitting on a bench overlooking the lake broadcasting angry, ranting talk radio, which seemed a poor choice and a profaning of the day. And then there was me, speech-to-texting this essay with the waves crashing below and the wind whipping all around, trying not to bother anybody, but perhaps, even I was committing some oblivious human blunder, disturbing a sleeping wood butterfly perhaps, with my musings.

If I tell people I consider certain trees, hummingbirds, the lakeshore, certain birds my friends, they might wonder if I have enough human friends--maybe, maybe not. All I know is that these living creatures are also my friends, and I feel close to them. Fellow humans might point out that friendship involves some sort of give and take. So what are trees and lakeshores and hummingbirds asking of me? It's obvious they ask what any living thing asks for. To be noticed. To be seen and not judged. To be appreciated. I cannot think of a better definition of friendship, anyway.

Fellow humans may ask, "how do you know these creatures feel the same way about you?" I do not know for sure how they feel about me: but do you know for sure how the humans in your life feel about you? Studies show many of the people we consider our friends do not feel the same level of affection or attachment for us. Sometimes they don't even feel reciprocal friendship for us at all.

I'm sure we've all been on both sides of that equation.

Instinct tells me that the odds are as good with nature as they are with humans. Perhaps better.

It's a risk I am willing to take.

---

[i] See, for example, "*Staying Autistic, Staying Feral*" by Amy Gaeta

Feathers
Karen Pierce Gonzalez

FICTION

Languages Where Green And Blue Are One Colour

Amanda McLeod

(an ekphrastic response to Georgia O'Keeffe's 1918 painting, *Blue Flower*)

Layers of silk swish and rub against Sophie's bare body, like the fingertips of an impatient lover. She lifts the hem of the overskirt and gazes at the understory, the layers from ice blue and seafoam, deepening in chroma and value through ultramarine and sapphire, viridian and emerald. The bodice hugs her ribs and hips like nacre on a pearl, and flares just a little lower than is acceptable; while the neckline reveals the small freckle at the base of her sternum. This piece of haute couture is less a hint at what is beneath it than a neon sign.

Her dresser carefully levers Sophie into the gown, using a crochet needle to knit the bead buttons together down her spine. Sophie slides her fingers around to the nape of her neck and lifts her hair up, letting the air conditioning cool her before lowering her blonde curls. She steps into the canary yellow stilettos and eyes herself in the mirror one last time. Which layer of the underskirt is the exact same colour as her eyes? She can't decide. But she knows that all the hues of her dress will stand out on the red carpet, calling like siren song.

The red carpet, and the flashes pop as Sophie lights up to greet them. Step out of the car, knees together, nobody else needs to know she's only wearing one thing. Jewellery doesn't count. The diamond bracelet on her wrist sparkles as Sophie puts a hand on one hip, showing it off. Step, step, smile, and pose, throw that shoulder back. Behind her she can hear her co-star's arrival - the screams take on a desperate hysteria. He follows her up the red carpet, stalking his prey, always just behind. On the steps of the theatre they meet. His eyes devour her as she kicks out the hem of the dress, giving the photographers a glimpse of the dichromatic layers beneath. They stand together, answering questions about the film, flattering each other, with his arm around her waist, his hand resting in the curve between her ribcage and hipbone. He leans in, whispers a question. Sophie laughs, the perfect actress. As they turn and enter the theatre, she answers him with a single word. *Nothing.*

After, when he's left her in the bathroom stall with a kiss and a Xanax, Sophie smoothes down the layers of the dress, looking at all the blues and greens. She swallows the Xanax, and thinks about how blue and green mean fidelity and permission. The diamond bracelet her husband gave her glitters like ice in the dark. It'll be in all the newspapers in the morning.

Cup and Straws
Karen Pierce Gonzalez

CONTRIBUTORS

Sandy Benitez

Poetry — Medusa

Sandy Benitez writes lyrical poetry & fiction, sometimes dark, magical, or mysterious. Her fondest memories of childhood are from her years in Germany, playing in the vast woods behind her home which contributed to her lifelong love of fairy tales, magical realism, and the paranormal. Sandy currently resides in Southern California with her husband and two children.

Leslie Cairns

Poetry — The Daisies Miss Me

Leslie holds an MA English degree from SUNY Fredonia. She currently lives in Denver, and enjoys writing about nature, dementia, and mental health. She has upcoming poetry in Coffeezinemag as well as the Fiery Scribe Review. She's recently published in Honeyguide Magazine, Ilinix Magazine, and Silent Spark Press. Twitter: starbucksgirly

Alexander Etheridge

Poetry — With the Birds Again

Alexander Etheridge has been developing his poems and translations since 1998. His poems have been featured in Wilderness House Literary Review, Ink Sac, Cerasus Journal, The Cafe Review, The Madrigal, Abridged Magazine, Susurrus Magazine, The Journal, and many others. He was the winner of the Struck Match Poetry Prize in 1999.

K. Gene Friedman

Creative Non-Fiction — Bundles of Three
K. Gene Friedman is a queer, invisibly disabled high school dropout working in sexual and reproductive health. Her words appear in Maudlin House, Entropy, Expat Press, and Queen Mob's Tea House. Future Tense Books will publish her chapbook Foreign Body in November, 2022. You can find her on Twitter @ValleyGirlLift.

Karen Pierce Gonzalez

Visual Art — Feather, Pine Burst, Cup and Straws, Enchanted Forest, Black Swan (cover)
Karen Pierce Gonzalez's mixed-media assemblages (and collages) are always a layered conversation with the natural elements of this world. 'When I listen to the grain of tree bark, the contours of textiles, and the waters of color, I hear many songs worth singing.'
Art exhibits include Santa Rosa Arts Center, Sebastopol Center for the Arts, Tiny Galleries Kiosk, Truckenbrod Gallery, Virtual Art in the Park and FERAL: A Journal of Poetry and Art. She is also a published writer, poet, and folklorist who lives in the San Francisco Bay Area.

John Grey

Poetry - Rains Me

John Grey is an Australian poet, US resident, recently published in Sheepshead Review, Stand, Poetry Salzburg Review and Hollins Critic. Latest books, "Leaves On Pages" "Memory Outside The Head" and "Guest Of Myself" are available through Amazon. Work upcoming in Ellipsis, Blueline and International Poetry Review.

Grant Howington

Poetry - Hiraeth

Grant Howington is somebody who enjoys wearing many hats both figurative and literal. Born and raised in Michigan, by day he is a bookkeeper for a Detroit non-profit organization. He spends his evenings reading, writing, making music and visual art, or falling down rabbit holes on Wikipedia. Grant enjoys spending free-time with his family, including his girlfriend, and dog. He writes to feel and find his connections to the world.

Margaret King

Creative Non-Fiction - An autistic reflects on friendship with trees, lakes, and certain birds

Margaret King enjoys penning poetry, flash fic, and micro essays. Her recent work has appeared in MoonPark Review, Sledgehammer, and Moist Poetry Journal. In 2021, she was nominated for a Pushcart for her eco-flash fiction story "The Sky Is Blue." She teaches tai chi in Wisconsin. She is also the author of the poetry collection, Isthmus.

Richard LeDue

Poetry - Fallen

Richard LeDue (he/him) currently lives in Norway House, Manitoba. He is a Best of the Net nominee. He is the author of three chapbooks and two full length poetry collections. His latest collection, "Dollar Store Blues and Other Cheap Words," was released in March 2022 from Alien Buddha Press.

Rob McKinnon

Poetry - The Open Door

Rob McKinnon lives in the Adelaide Hills, South Australia. His poetry has previously been published in 'Adelaide: Mapping the Human City' Ginninderra Press, 'Messages from the Embers' Black Quill Press, Backstory Journal (Swinburne University), The Saltbush Review (Adelaide University), Nightingale and Sparrow, Wales Haiku Journal, and other online and print journals.

Amanda McLeod

Fiction - Languages Where Green And Blue Are One Colour

Amanda McLeod is a Canberra based writer and artist. Her work has appeared in many places both in print and online, including EcoTheo Review and Wild Roof Journal. A lover of quiet and wild places, she's usually outside.

John C. Polles

Poetry - quiet, quiet, quiet

John C. Polles is a copyeditor from Northeast
Ohio whose creative work has appeared in —
or is forthcoming from — Rubbertop Review,
Wyrd & Wyse, Queerlings, Kissing Dynamite,
and more. A graduate of Kent State University
at Stark, he previously served as Editor-in-Chief
of Canto: A Magazine for Literature & Art. In
his spare time, John enjoys working with local
marching band and colorguard programs.

Daniel Rabuzzi

*Creative Non-Fiction - A Flowing Drop
Suspended In Time, Still Flowing*

Daniel A. Rabuzzi has had two novels, five
short stories and twenty poems published
(www.danielarabuzzi.com). He lived eight years
in Norway, Germany and France, and earned
degrees in the study of folklore and mythology,
and European history. He lives in New York
City with his artistic partner & spouse, the
woodcarver Deborah A. Mills
(www.deborahmillswoodcarving.com), and the
requisite cat. Tweets @TheChoirBoats

John Rodzvilla

Poetry - Astronomy Two Ways

John Rodzvilla teaches in the Publishing and
Writing programs at Emerson College in
Boston. His work has appeared in Harvard
Review, McSweeney's Internet Tendency,
gorse, DecomP, Verbatim and Bad Robot
Poetry.

Jeffrey Yamaguchi

Visual art - A Found Poem from a Never Returned Book

Jeffrey Yamaguchi is a writer, poet, and photographer exploring and experimenting in the field of book publishing.

ISSUE STAFF

Juliette Sebock
Founding Editor

Juliette Sebock (she/her) is a Best of the Net-nominated poet and writer and the author of *Mistakes Were Made* (2017), *Micro* (2019), *How My Cat Saved My Life and Other Poems* (2019), *Plight of the Pangolin* (2020), *Three Words* (2020) and ^ (2020), with work forthcoming or appearing in a wide variety of publications. Currently, she is working on a variety of personal and freelance projects. When she isn't writing (and sometimes when she is), Juliette can be found with a cup of coffee and her cat, Fitz. Juliette can be reached via her website (juliettesebock.com) or across social media (@juliettesebock).

Marcelle Newbold
Managing Editor

Marcelle Newbold's poetry explores place and inheritance. Pushcart Prize nominated, and winner of the Poetry in the Arcades competition in 2020, her poems have been published in online and print magazines including *Ink Sweat & Tears*, *Iamb poet*, and *The Ekphrastic Review*. Her writing has featured in recent print anthologies by *Black Bough Poetry, Maytree Press, Wild Pressed Books, Icefloe Press,* and *Indigo Dreams.* Marcelle lives in Cardiff, Wales where she trained as an architect. Linktree: marcellenewbold

Alina Melnik
Head Curator

Alina Melnik is a writer from the Pacific Northwest. She loves literature and art and enjoys exploring how the two can intersect.

Fija Callaghan
Fiction Editor (she/her)

Fija Callaghan is a storyteller who writes poetry, love letters, and fiction that can be found in a range of literary journals and magazines in print and across the web. You might see her sitting in a café with a notebook, sunning on the docks of the Portobello Canal, or looking out at the sea and wondering what it would be like to have fins.

Paige Lalain
Head CNF Editor

Paige Lalain is a Best of the Net-nominated essayist and professional editor based in Michigan's thumb. She has a degree in creative writing with a specialization in literary nonfiction from Oakland University. A Creative Writing for Therapeutic Purposes (CWTP) practitioner, Paige has guest lectured in a master's program and held workshops with people in the U.S. and abroad. Paige's passion is helping others write, reflect on, take pride in, and make peace with their personal narratives.

Scout Roux
Fiction Editor

Scout Roux is a Wisconsin writer of fiction and poetry. Their work can be found in *Wild Roof Journal*, *Passengers Journal*, and *Barstow & Grand*, among others. They live a quiet life of pancake flipping and transcription with their partner and two cats. Tweets @scoutroux

Made in the USA
Monee, IL
20 August 2022

12035040R00036